Modern Curriculum Press
BEGINNING
TO
READ
Series

# MODERN CURRICULUM PRESS

# Who Said That?

Alvin Granowsky
Joy Ann Tweedt
Craig L. Tweedt
Illustrated by Michael L. Denman

MODERN CURRICULUM PRESS
Cleveland • Toronto

© **1985 MODERN CURRICULUM PRESS, INC.**
13900 Prospect Road, Cleveland, Ohio 44136.

Softcover edition published simultaneously in Canada by Globe/
Modern Curriculum Press, Toronto.

**Library of Congress Cataloging in Publication Data**

Granowsky, Alvin, 1936-
    Who said that?

    Summary: Mrs. Miller plans to surprise her class with a talking
computer, but the class gets to the computer first and has a nice
surprise for the teacher.

    1. Children's stories, American. (1. Schools — Fiction.
2. Computers — Fiction.     3. Birthdays — Fictional)
I. Tweedt, Craig, 1950-      .     II. Tweedt, Joy, 1951-
III. Denman, Michael L., ill.     IV. Title.
PZ7.G76664Wh     1985     (E)     84-9001

ISBN  0-8136-5142-5 (hardcover)
ISBN  0-8136-5642-7 (paperback)

4 5 6 7 8 9 10     89  90  91  92

"Tomorrow we will have a surprise!"
said Mrs. Miller.
"It will be a wonderful surprise!"

"What is the surprise?"
Could it be something to eat?"

"Could it be someone on TV?
Could it be a trip with the class?"

Dave ran to school.
"Today I will see the surprise!"

9

# "Who said good morning to me?"

"The new computer said it!
This is the surprise," said Joy.
"We have a talking computer!"

11

"I told it your name.
This is how you do it.
You type in the name."

"That looks like fun!" said Dave.
"Let me tell the computer a name.
I will type JOHN."

"I am not John!
I am Mary.
Who called me JOHN?"

"It is the talking computer!
The computer called you JOHN."

"The computer does not know that!
You have to tell it," said Dave.
"Look. I will type your name."

"Oh, I like that!" said Mary.
"The computer can say my name!
What a wonderful surprise!
We have a talking computer!"

"We can surprise Mrs. Miller!"
said Joy.
"It is her birthday today.
I have a birthday cake for her."

"The new computer can talk to Mrs. Miller.
We can tell it what to say.
We can make it say, HAPPY BIRTHDAY!"

"The new computer said it.
We have a talking computer!
This is the surprise.
See how it works?" said Mary.

"Who said that?" said Mrs. Miller.

"Surprise!" said the children.
"Happy birthday!" said the children.

"I wanted to surprise you with
the talking computer.
But you have surprised me!"
said Mrs. Miller.
"What a happy birthday for me!"

# WHO SAID THAT?

Word Count: 77
Readability: 1.5

| | | | |
|---|---|---|---|
| a | happy | name | the |
| am | have | new | this |
| ~ | her | not | to |
| be | how | | today |
| birthday | | oh | told |
| but | I | on | tomorrow |
| | in | | trip |
| cake | is | Pat | TV |
| called | it | | type |
| can | | ran | |
| children | Joy | | wanted |
| class | John | said | we |
| computer | | say | what |
| could | know | school | who |
| | | see | will |
| Dave | let | someone | with |
| did | like | something | wonderful |
| do | look(s) | surprise(d) | works |
| does | | | |
| | make | talk(ing) | you |
| eat | Mary | tell | your |
| | me | that | |
| for | Miller | | |
| fun | morning | | |
| | Mrs. | | |
| good | my | | |